# MY HOME

## Heather Fontaine-Youngs

Order this book online at www.trafford.com
or email orders@trafford.com

Most Trafford titles are also available at major online book retailers.

 www.trafford.com

**North America & international**
toll-free: 844 688 6899 (USA & Canada)
fax: 812 355 4082

Our mission is to efficiently provide the world's finest, most comprehensive book publishing service, enabling every author to experience success. To find out how to publish your book, your way, and have it available worldwide, visit us online at www.trafford.com

ISBN: 978-1-6987-1058-7 (sc)
ISBN: 978-1-6987-1057-0 (e)

Print information available on the last page.

Trafford rev. 12/09/2021

# My Home

By
HEATHER FONTAINE-YOUNGS

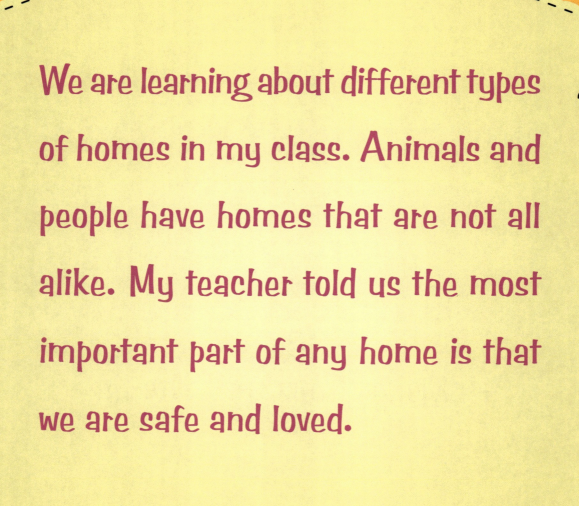

We are learning about different types of homes in my class. Animals and people have homes that are not all alike. My teacher told us the most important part of any home is that we are safe and loved.

A *home* is a place where people live *permanently* (that means all the time) and a *shelter* is a place that gives temporary protection (that means for a short time) from outside.

People live in homes like houses or apartment buildings like my classmates.

I live in a shelter. It's called the Open Hearts and Arms shelter. A shelter is home for people that don't have their own *permanent* home yet. I live here with my mom. It is my home…for now.

There are different reasons people have to live in shelters. I used to live in an apartment building. But it caught on fire.

We all got out safely but all I was able to take with me was my Bear. I miss my room, but I know I will have a new home and room soon.

Here at Open Hearts and Arms, there are other families like mine. I have made new friends here but some have gone to move into their new very own *permanent* homes.

We got good news today! We are moving into our new home!

I learned that there are different kinds of homes and as long as I am safe and loved, that is all that matters.

Printed in the United States
by Baker & Taylor Publisher Services